W. Holland

Sibelle or up among the Millions

A Society Drama, in Five Acts

W. Holland

Sibelle or up among the Millions
A Society Drama, in Five Acts

ISBN/EAN: 9783743444096

Printed in Europe, USA, Canada, Australia, Japan

Cover: Foto ©Andreas Hilbeck / pixelio.de

Manufactured and distributed by brebook publishing software
(www.brebook.com)

W. Holland

Sibelle or up among the Millions

SIBELLE;

OR,

Up Among the Millions

A SOCIETY DRAMA,

IN FIVE ACTS.

By W. HOLLAND.

LONGMONT, COLO.:
VALLEY HOME AND FARM PRINT.

1879.

CAST OF CHARACTERS:

SIBELLE, a Millionaire,...*Miss Libbie Tiffany*
CLARENCE SUMMERFIELD, in love with Sibelle,.....................*W. Holland*
EUGENE WATSON, after Sibelle's money,.............................*F. Salade*
EDA THORNTON, in love with Eugene,.......................*Miss Mary Boynton*
MR. PARTINGTON, Detective, in disguise as a Swell,.....................*W. Cole*
BOBBY BURT, Eugene Watson's confederate.........................*S. Williams*
MR. HOWELL, Clergyman,...*J. J. Burke*
ALICE JEWETT, Guest of Sibelle,................ ....*Miss Ida Holland*
LULU MUNGER,   "   "   ....*Miss Evelyn Cole*
CECIL COLLINS,   "   "   ....*C. F. Kendall*
LEROY ALLEN,   "   "   ....*A. L. Williams*
Old PHILIP, Servant (colored),.............................. .....*C. W. Boynton*
JOHN, Footman,... ....*M. Wilson*

COSTUMES.

SIBELLE : ACT I., Fashionably attired. ACT II., **first dress, velvet riding
habit, blue or black** ; second dress, fashionable attire for evening
party, with summer shawl and hat. ACTS III., IV. and V., fashionably
attired
EDA THORNTON : ACT I., Fashionably attired. ACT II. Evening party
dress. ACTS III., IV. and V., dressed in fashion.
MISS MUNGER : ACT II., Evening party. ACT III. Dressed in fashion.
MISS JEWETT: ACT II., Evening party. ACT III., Dressed in fashion.
MESSRS. COLLINS and ALLEN : ACT II., **Evening party.** ACT III., in
fashion.
MR. PARTINGTON : Light pants and vest, light wig and light side whiskers. lavender kid gloves and cane, eye glasses and large button hole
boquet.
EUGENE WATSON : ACT I , In fashion. ACT II., **Evening party.** All other
acts in fashion.
CLARENCE SUMMERFIELD : ACT I., In fashion. ACT II., Wretchedly
clad. All other acts, in fashion,
MR. HOWELL.: Black clothes, white cravat. black silk hat, gray hair and
whiskers, cloak black.
BOBBY BURT: Checkered pants, blue or green vest, black coat, striped
shirt and collar, flashy neck tie. white silk hat. loud kid gloves, cane,
dark mustache and heavy black eyebrows.
Old PHILIP: Black swallow-tail coat, white low cut vest, black pants.
gray side whiskers and wig.
JOHN: Brown or blue dress coat close fitting light pants, buff top boots,
standing white collar, white neck-tie, white gloves, black silk hat.

LIST OF PROPERTIES.

ACT I.: Two letters and photograph for Clarence ; Album, three boquets.
box, supposed to contain fruit painting of an old man, for Philip ; white
and red rose, for Sibelle ; white and red rose, for Eugene and Clarence to
wear in button hole; dust brush. ACT II.: Pistol, not loaded. for Clarence ;
bottle, supposed to contain drugged whiskey, for Eugene: dirk knife for
Eugene ; saddle horse for Sibelle; letter for Philip. ACT III.: Chess and
checkerboard. tray, wine and wine glasses containing wine; dust brush ;
dirk knife for Clarence ; book of poems for Sibelle. ACT IV.: Letter for
Clarence ; pistol. not loaded. for Eugene. ACT V.: Handkerchief for
Sibelle ; two pistols, loaded with blank cartridges, for Clarence and
Eugene.

STAGE DIRECTIONS.

R. means Right of Stage, facing the Audience ; L. Left ; C. Centre ; R. C.
Right of Centre ; L. C. Left of Centre ; D. F. Door in the Flat. or Scene
running across the back of the Stage ; C D. F. Centre Door in the Flat ;
R. D. F. Right Door in the Flat ; L. D. F. Left Door in the Flat ; R. D. Right
Door ; L. D. Left Door ; 1 E. First Entrance ; 2 E. Second Entrance ; U. E.
Upper Entrance ; 1, 2 or 3 G. First. Second or Third Groove.

R.   R. C.   C.   L. C.   L.

☞ The reader is supposed to be upon the stage facing the audience.

SIBELLE.

SEASON OF PLAY: Summer.

ACT I.

TIME—*Day.*

SCENE 1. *An elegantly furnished drawing room; satin damask and lace window curtains; two sofettes, and chairs covered with satin, marble top table with large boquet of flowers, books, album, etc.; large mirror (back centre), resting on marble slab; piano* L.*; fine blue or red exminster carpet, curtains and furniture to match; gold tinted wall paper. Everything stylish. Door right of mirror in* F.*; window left of mirror in* F., *door* R. 2 E., *and door* L. 2 E. *Curtain rises.*

Enter PHILIP, *whistling, with Mr. Saunders picture and dust brush,* D. F.

Philip. Law sakes alive! I never seed so much company as Miss Sibelle has! heah de picture of old Massa Saunders, her husband. Sibelle is a mighty nice young lady to go and marry sich a dried up little ole man [*shakes his head*]. Pears mighty strange how de ole man done left dis world [*hangs up picture*]. Now if she'd done married Massa Eugene, or Massa Clarence, I wouldn't been so tickler bout de case; but to go and marry a little dried up ole man—humph! pshaw! Ole Phil knowed dar would come no good of sich doins. Ole Massa done treated Missis mighty bad, I tell you, so one bright sunshiny morning de ole man woke up dead—dis as dead as dis brush dat I holds in my hand. [*Scratching his head.*] I speck some one done draped pizen in his coffee. If dat is so, de pint is to find out who draped it Ole Phil dont know—dont know nuffin bout it; but den it wouldn't do for all dem ignorant sassy niggers dat ole Massa used to have on de plantation to know what ole Phil knows, kase dar mought be trouble. Ever time Miss Sibelie is gwine to have company, she say " Philip, de picture ;" I says, "Yes, marm," and goes right straight add totes it to her room. Mighty hard to keep tings in order in dis room. I guess dat will do.

[*Exit, whistling* L. D.]

[*Enter* SIBELLE, R. D., *and looking sadly, and sits at table,* C.]

Sibelle. "Oh, what a sad, unhappy life I have led! When but a small child, stolen from my dear father and mother, from a home of plenty, where peace and harmony, in happy concord reigned supreme. I never will forget my mother: her tender look; her mild blue eyes; her gentle smile; her fond and devoted love! Oh, who but the orphan can know what it is to be deprived of home, of father, mother, sister, brother—to miss their affections—their love! What can compensate for loss of motner? who can fill a mother's place? no one—no one! My marriage proved unhappy; and, owing to my husband's mysterious death, I was tried for the murder. I left for the south, thinking I would live a retired life, but visitors will crowd themselves upon me, and the constant fear of having my secret disclosed, is dreadful.

[*Rings bell, enter* D. *in* F.]

Phil. Yes, marm. You dont know what Sarah tole me dis morning bout your har, she says you had such nice har, and dat dem fowers you wears do so become you. I tinks so too, Miss Sibelle—dey looks dis like de flowers you used to bring home from de plantation. I tole Sarah as she had not been heah long, to take my advice and not ax too many questions. [*Sibelle is looking at Saunder's picture.*] Miss Sibelle, what makes you look at de ole man so much?

Sibelle. Why, Philip! How dare you be so impertinent, and make use of such expressions? sir, leave the room!

Phil. Yes, marm.   [*Exit* D. F.]

Sibelle. Philip is getting to be very rude. It will not do - I must check him of his familiarity, or he will be unmanag; able in a short time.   [*Rings bell, enter Philip.*]

Sibelle. Philip, I'm going to my room to take a nap, I am not feeling very well this morning. If any one calls, tell them I cannot see them.   [*Exit* L. D.]

Phil. Yes, marm. Dat Sarah was comin' heah to dress Miss Sibelle's har; didn't have any more sense dan to come to de drawing room ; she'll larn something if she stay about heah. [*Enter Sibelle,* L. D.] Isn't you gwine to take a nap, Miss Sibelle ?

Sibelle. No, I forgot. I have changed my mind; I am expecting some one; but, Philip, you must not be so inquisitive.

Phil. You does'nt look well, Miss Sibelle. What's de matter, chile, you isn't gwine to be sick, is you ?

Sibelle. I hope not—you can go, Philip; but stop—the picture.

Phil. Yes marm. [*Leaves with picture, and returns.*] Miss Sibelle, de ladies has called for de flowahs to take to de hospital.

Sibelle. Oh! yes [*taking two boquets off piano*], tell the ladies I am sorry that I cannot make my usual calls on the patients for several days, that I am feeling rather indisposed, and that I wish I had something more substantial to send them.

Phil. Yes, marm. [*Leaving.*]

Sibelle. Oh! I forgot. Here, Philip, is a box of fruit, that will be a little better.

Phil. Yes, marm. [*Exit with fruit and flowers, D. in F.*

Enter Eda Thornton and Eugene Watson, D. in F., Eda carrying a boquet

Sibelle. [*Aside.*] What! Eugene Watson with Eda Thornton?

Eda. Good morning, Sibelle.

Eugene. Good morning.

Sibelle. [*Shaking hands.*] Ah! how do you do, friends? I suppose you have had a pleasant walk, this morning?

Eda. Yes, it is a beautiful morning, the sun shines so brightly; not too warm, but pleasant; and the flowers in your garden do look beautiful. I think a morning ramble over your grounds, and the exhilarating air, quite beneficial.

Eugene. Yes, I found Miss Eda, gathering and arranging a boquet. She was kind enough to decorate my lapel with this red rose. [*Goes to piano, looks over music.*

Eda. How do you like my taste in the arrangement?

Sibelle. Oh, Eda, *you* have good taste in everything.

Eda. I will make you a present of it for your compliments.

Sibelle. Ah, thank you, Eda [*takes flowers*]. Now I will leave you for a few moments, you will excuse me, I suppose —enjoy yourselves. [*Exit R. D.*

Eugene. Do you play, Eda?

Eda. Not much [*going to piano*]. Excuse me a moment, Eugene, I will be back soon.

Eugene. Where are you going?

Eda. Oh, I'll be back soon.

Eugene. That is all right, but dont stay long. [*Plays with red rose, and lays it on piano.*] [*Exit, 1 E. L., EDA.*

Eugene. Well, this Sibelle is a very nice young lady, some would call her beautiful. Although I can never love her, I must win her for her wealth. A nice rich young lady is not to be picked up every day, and, as I have only a small salary, I cannot marry Eda, the only woman I ever loved. It will be hard to give her up; but I must do it.

Enter EDA, 1 E. L.

Eda. Were you talking just now, Eugene?

Eugene. [Starting with alarm.] No -yes—I was saying to myself—I mean I was thinking—I was anticipating the happiness in store for us, in the future.

Eda. Yes, but why so confused?

Eugene. Such an acknowledgement would confuse most any one, especially when intruded upon by such a pretty face as yours.

EDA *hangs her head,* EUGENE'S *arm around her waist, as* SIBELLE *appears at* D. *in* F., *but does not enter.*

Eda. [Disengages his arm.] Dont. Sibelle, you know.

Eugene. Oh, yes, she may be in at any moment.
[*They sit on Sofa. Enter* SIBELLE.

Sibelle. I only walked out in the garden. Have you enjoyed yourselves?

Eda. Oh, yes, *we* always enjoy ourselves.

Sibelle. [Looking meaningly at Eugene.] I should think two young people, like you, *ought* to enjoy each others company.

Enter CLARENCE SUMMERFIELD, *white rose on lapel of coat,*
D. F.

Sibelle. Ah, Mr. Summerfield, how do you do? Out for a walk?

Clarence. Yes, my physician's advice is exercise and fresh air. I find an improvement, I am happy to say, under that treatment. [SIBELLE *introduces* EDA *and* EUGENE; *they all bow.*

Eda. [All seated, CLARENCE *with* SIBELLE.] You have been confined to your room for some time, Mr. Summerfield. Do you think you will wholly recover?

Clarence. I think so, in time.

Sibelle. It is too bad you are lame, though I consider your partial recovery miraculous. I think I should have died, had I been in your condition; I think you must have an extraordinary amount of patience.

Clarence. We all have patience when necessity compels it. What a nice boquet that is! From your own garden, I suppose.

Sibelle. Yes, Eda and Mr. Watson—that is—Eda gathered it for me.

Clarence. [Going to table C.] Very tastefully arranged, very, very nice! [*Looking at Album.*]

Sibelle. I dont suppose you will know any of them.

Clarence. I like to look at albums; I always find them interesting. Isn't yours here?

Sibelle. No, I have none at present.

Eugene. I believe I will take a walk. I will leave you and Sibelle to entertain Mr. Summerfield while I am gone.
Exit D. F.

Sibelle. Have you any photographs? I would like to see some of your friends.

Clarence. Not many. I have one or two with me, come to think about it. [*Hands her photographs, leaves letters on table.*
Sibelle, [*Taking photographs.*] Thanks.

Enter PHILIP, D. F.

Phil. Heah is a letter, Miss Sibelle.   [*Hands it to her.*
          [*Exit*, D. F.
Clarence. While you read your letter, Miss Thornton and I will take a stroll, that is, providing she is willing.
Eda. [*Bowing.*] Certainly.
Sibelle. As you are lame, Mr. Summerfield, you must not try to be too gallant.
Clarence. I hope Miss Thornton will excuse any deficiency on my part.
Eda. Oh, of course.
          [*Exit* CLARENCE *and* EDA *arm in arm*, D. F.
Sibelle. Goodness! this is not for me! [*reads*] Mr. Ed. Saville. This is a mistake. [*Leaves letter on piano. Looks at photographs at table* C.] This is a nice looking gentleman, I wonder who he is? Ah! a young lady—rather pretty. [*Silently looks at the rest.*] What is this? Great Heavens! my mother's picture! How came he by it? What mystery is this? Ah, dear mother, it has been a long time since I saw thee last! What can this mean? [*Goes to sofa, hands to head, thinking. returns to table,* C.] Ah, what letters are these? [*reads*] Clarence Summerfield; [*reads another*] Will Hastings. What! Will Hastings, my brother! what can this mean? Oh, I see, Clarence is my brother; he has assumed the name of Summerfield. My own brother has proposed marriage! Oh, what will I tell him? how can I answer him? I cannot tell him I am his sister! No, the secret he *must not* know. Oh! this is horrible! Will the mystery ever be solved? [*Goes to piano, tak.s up two roses.*] Two flowers that lovingly entwine in each others embrace, and kiss the dew from each others petals that nourish them into faultless beauty. That is what Eugene wrote to me once, in describing some flowers. [*Holding up white.*] White denotes purity [*shakes her head*]. That is not for me. [*Takes red rose.*] This is the one Eugene wore; *this* is the one for me.
          [CLARENCE *appears at door in* F. *during the last sentence.*

Enter CLARENCE, D. F.

Clarence. [*Arm around her.*] Sibelle, you are not in very good spirits.
Sibelle. Oh, Clarence, I feel *so* unhappy !
Clarence. Why so sad, what is the trouble? are you sick ?
Sibelle. No, I can't say I am sick, although I am not feeling very well.
Clarence. I did not expect to find you in such a mood; I think I have come in at the wrong time.

Sibelle. Why so.

Clarence. Because, I have come to ask you if you have decided in the matter.

Sibelle. Mr. Summerfield, I can never be your wife.

Clarence. What, Sibelle! you can never be my wife? why not?

Sibelle. I cannot—I—Oh! do not ask me!

Clarence. Oh, I think I can explain—this is the rose that Eugene wore, *this* is the one for me.

Sibelle. No, no, no! you do *not* understand.

Clarence. I *think* I understand.

Sibelle. You do not.

Clarence. Sibelle, do you know why I wore that white rose? Because the first flower you ever gave me was a small white rose.

Sibelle. I have often thought of that.

Clarence. I thought the doner of that white rose would have me understand that she was pure—as white denotes purity—I did think so, but I find I have been deceived. Is it true that you have no special regard for me? Sibelle, I had entertained a higher opinion of you than to believe you could so lower your noble nature, and participate in such a scurvy deception. I have always looked to you as a sample of unsullied virtue, having a soul with all the finer and nobler qualities of true womanhood, that would not stoop to betray a trust or stain her honor.

Sibelle. You are highly regarded in my estimation, more so, perhaps, than a mere friend would be, but I see I have done wrong to encourage you. Thus far I explain—no farther. I beseech you, leave me awhile until I collect my scattered thoughts.

Clarence. One word : is it indeed true, you will not be my wife?

Sibelle. It is; but I implore you use no reproaches, for beneath the attesting eye of Heaven I vow I mean you no wrong ; and I would blush to have tarnished that which is most sacred to woman—her honor.

Clarence. Yet it is very plain you have deceived me!

Sibelle. Oh, no sir, circumstances brought about the deception. I was no willing partner in the act. Believe me, I am innocent ; and I hope you will sometimes think of me kindly. You may yet be satisfied in the love of some true and noble woman.

Clarence. No, no—None but Sibelle can fill the place of the ideal woman my soul most cherished. No ill feelings lie silently buried in the deep recesses of my heart. I will always think kindly of you. I sincerely hope your future life may be peaceful and happy; that no adverse winds will blow a storm to ruffle the usual serenity of your gentle spirit; that you may continue in your benevolent purpose, and may the blessings of Heaven be bounteously showered upon you.

Sibelle. I assure you your good wishes are reciprocated. I can only thank you for your kind generosity.

Clarence. With this I quit you; Sibelle, farewell forever.

Sibelle. Oh, Clarence, say not those words. You do not know what you say—you do not understand. Recall those words, Clarence, do not leave me forever!

Clarence. Then I will say, good bye, until I see you again.

Sibelle. You will call again?

Clarence. Yes; but to see you become another man's wife, I should go mad. Good bye.

Sibelle. Good bye. [*Exit* CLARENCE, D. F.] Oh! was there ever woman in such trouble? I cannot tell him! What will I do?

SCENE 2. *Ordinary room in* 1st G. *Enter Clarence,* L. 1 E.

Clarence. Oh, how long the past two weeks have been. Slowly the weary hours drag on. Never did I feel the need of a companion more than now. Never did the dark clouds hang more thickly around me. This loneliness is becoming unendurable! Oh, for some one to cheer me in my hours of gloom and adversity.

Enter EDA, L. 1 L.

Eda. Ah, you are here, Clarence! I was surprised when Sarah told me you wished to see me, you generally like to be alone.

Clarence. I sent for you because I feel that I need your presence. Oh, Eda, you dont know the influence of a refined lovely woman! Place her among the flowers, foster her as a tender plant, and she is a thing of fancy—annoyed by a dew drop, fretted by the touch of a butterfly's wings, ready to faint at the rattle of a window pane. She is overpowered by the perfume of a rose bud. But let real calamity come, rouse her affections, enkindle the fires of her heart, and mark her then! How strong is her heart! Place her in the seat of battle—give her a child, a bird or anything to protect, and see her, lifting her white arms as a shield, while praying for life to protect the helpless. Transplant her to the dark places of the earth, call forth her energies to action, and her presence becomes a blessing. She disputes inch by inch, the strides of a stalking pestilence, when man, the strong and brave, pale, affrighted, shrinks away. Misfortune haunts her not. In prosperity, she is a bud full of odors; in

short, woman is a miracle, a mystery from which radiates
the charm of existence.

Eda. You are very complimentary to the women.

Clarence. Nevertheless 'tis true. Eda, I am weary of leading this lonely life. I feel, greatly, the need of a companion
for life, and I ask you openly and frankly will you be my
wife?

Eda. Why Clarence—this is so sudden—I really—you
must give me time to consider.

Clarence. Consider? No. Now, Eda, now.

Eda. Not even until to-night?

Clarence. Not even until to-night. Now, before we part
company, will it be yes, or no?

Eda. Yes.

Clarence. Then, [*takes her hands,*] hand in hand we will
fight the battle of life, and o'er the rugged path strew flowers
to make our burdens more lightsome.

Enter PHILIP, R. 1 E., *exit* EDA *and* CLARENCE L. 1 E., CLARENCE'S
arm around her.

Phil. I declar if dar aint Miss Eda and Mistah Summerfield. Its de mixtus up afar I evah seed. First, its Eda and
Eugene, den its Eugene and Sibelle, now its Eda and Clarence. I dosn't know which is which. Dar, [*looking* L.,] he's
got his arm around her. [*Scratches his head.*] Dont 'peer to
me like dey is 'havin zackly right. [*Bell rings.*] Dar's de
bell.   [*Exit* L. 1 E.

SCENE III. *Same as Scene I.* SIBELLE *seated at table, reading.*

Enter PHILIP, 1 E. L., *backward.*

Phil. Go 'way from me, man, dont pester wid me, kase if
you does, I'll spile your beauty—I'll bruise you.

Sibelle. What is the trouble, Philip?

Phil. Nuffin, dat English groom tryin' to kick up a muss,
and if he fools aruund ole Phil he,s gwine to get molested,
sure as you are born.

Sibelle. Have you seen Miss Thornton within the last few
hours?

Phil. Done seed her dis minute, in de parlor wid Massa
Summerfield. 'Pears like Massa talkin' mighty sweet, too.
Had his arm around her neck.

Sibelle. [*With surprise.*] Did he?

Phil. He did, for a fack.

Sibelle. You can go, Philip.

Phil. [*Bowing.*] Yes, marm.   [*Exit*, 1 E. L.

Enter EDA THORNTON, D. F.

Eda. Why, Sibelle, you are looking so sad. What is the matter, any bad news?

Sibelle. No—not exactly —I am not feeling very well.

Eda. Cheer up, I have some good news to tell you, that is, concerning myself.

Sibelle. What is it, Eda? you know I am always interested in your welfare, and would be happy to hear any good news concerning you.

Eda. Well, Sibelle, I am going to be married in a few days.

Sibelle. Ah! you were very sly about it. I suppose Mr. Watson is your choice.

Eda. No, gracious, no! He is not rich, you know, and the man that I marry must have money. But Eugene is awful nice, I tell you he is sweet.

Sibelle. Not Mr. Watson!

Eda. No, not Mr. Watson.

Sibelle. Eda, do you love this man you are engaged to?

Eda. No, I can't say I love him, but I will try and be happy with his money.

Sibelle. Do you think he could be happy under those circumstances?

Eda. I don't know as to that; but I can't help it, whether he will be or not; in fact, I don't care whether he is happy or not, I'll look out for No. 1.

Sibelle. May I ask who the gentleman is?

Eda. Yes; and you must not be surprised when I say it is Mr. Summerfield, the young millionaire.

Sibelle. What! my—my Clarence?

Eda. Why, Sibelle, is he anything to you?

Sibelle. Yes—no—I mean—no, he is nothing to me.

Eda. Oh, I understand. I believe I will go to my room.   [*Exit* EDA, L. D.

Sibelle. I am glad Eugene is free from that woman; but then my brother! She does not love him—oh! Clarence, I know you d) not love her. No, it must not be. I must save him from a miserable life. Oh! could I explain—could I tell him I am his sister!. How shall I act in the matter?

Enter EUGENE, D. F.

Eugene. Ah! you are looking sad, Sibelle, cheer up; it makes me feel bad to see you thus.

Sibelle. I wish to be alone, if you please.

Eugene. Well, good bye. I will see you again soon.   [*Exit* 1 E. L.

Enter CLARENCE, D. F.

Sibelle. Oh, Clarence, I am so glad you have come, I wanted so much to see you.

Clarence. [*Earnestly.*] Are you, Sibelle ?

Sibelle. Clarence, your future happiness is in danger, when coupled with that woman you are engaged to. I beg of you, do not marry her.

Clarence. What material difference can it make to you who I marry ?

Sibelle. I had not thought of that.

Clarence. It is very evident that you still have some interest in me.

Sibelle. Believe me, Clarence, she does not love you. You will be so unhappy—I implore, as one greatly interested in you, do not marry her! [EUGENE *appears at* D. *in* F.] Promise me you will not. Will you not promise, Clarence?

Clarence. I promise.   [SIBELLE'S *arm around his neck.*

Enter EUGENE, D. *in* F.

Eugene. What does this mean ? I do not understand it.

Clarence. It means that I'll have satisfaction—satisfaction !
[*Curtain.*

END OF ACT I.

ACT II.

TIME—*Night.*

SCENE 1. *Exterior front view of a beautiful dwelling,* L., *with veranda with heavy balustrade, and steps leading up, and balcony above. Imitation of green grass in front of house, heavy balustrade across stage, on stone foundation, with gateway in center. Two lamp posts, one on either side of gateway ; lamps lighted, woods, statuary and rustic seat,* R., *walk commencing at* 1st E. R., *running in a half circle and ending in* R. U. E.; *walk from gateway intersecting first walk. Flower pots and plants tastefully arranged ; hills, cascade and river scene for a background. Moon shines in sky. Curtain rises.*

Enter seven or eight couple of ladies and gentlemen by walk, R. U. E., *ring door bell, and exit in house. Enter brass band, and play in front of house. Company enter from house, and sit or stand during the music. After music, exit band and company in house. Enter* SIBELLE *on horse back, outside of fence, and stops at gateway.*
Enter JOHN *and hands her down.*

Sibelle. Have the guests arrived ?

John. Yes, ma'm.

Sibelle. I was detained longer than I expected. I am glad Eda was here to receive them. You can take Prince to the stable, and have the carriage ready in an hour.

John. Yes, ma'm. [*Exit* SIBELLE *in house.* JOHN *with horse* L.

Enter CLARENCE, R. U. E., *wretchedly clad; low music within.*

Clarence. 'Tis the festive night! Music and revelry within! Ah, happy hearts, dance and be merry, for you know not how soon the hard hand of fate may bow you in grief. How cool the gentle breeze! Yonder the cascade goes jumping o'er the adamantine rocks. Those antique hills clothed in their verdant robes! All seem beautiful and happy. Oh, what a contrast to a miserable aching heart! Even the moon shines more brightly, as if to mock me in my misery—make me more wretched by the recollections this scene calls forth. It hasn't changed since I saw it last. How often have I strolled over these grounds with Sibelle!—right over there she gathered flowers that soothed my hours of melancholly. But 'tis past—all past—those days are gone forever! How different now—no friends, no money—nothing! Nothing left but my poor miserable self, to drag out the long weary hours in bitter reflection! In my sober senses all this comes back to me. Oh! I must not think of it, 'twill drive me mad! 'twill drive me mad! Oh, could I sleep and silence grief; for on yester night I saw the moon go down at early morn; the thoughts of her did act like a feather tickling, that put to flight my quiet sleep; so cunning did they play their tricks.

Enter OLD PHILIP, L., *by walk, with letter.*

Phil. [*Looks at letter and scratches his head.*] I wonder who's dat done write to me! Who would go and write to ole Phil, who hasn't got no larnin' nor edication eader. I speck its some no account niggah tryin' to show off dar larnin. He—he—he—done knows morn ole Phil if he can read dat. Dem letters looks like little nigs jumpin' over a rail fence—he—he! somebody mus think heap sight of de ole man. Yes, but who is gwine to read it for me? dar's a pint. [*Looks around and sees* CLARENCE.] My sakes! dat man looks like he'd been drinkin' too much soda water. I'll dis ax him to read it. [*Goes to Clarence and bows.*] How de do, sah? please read dis letter for me, sah?

Clarence. Yes, old man, I will read it for you.

Phil. Thank you, sah—thank you sah.

Clarence. [*Takes letter and looks at it.*] Well sir, it is signed, "Aunt Judy Clemens."

Phil. Well, now, hear dat—hear dat. Aunt Judy, dat used to work for Judge Rently. Whar she now?

Clarence. [*Reading.*] "Philadelphia, June 4th."

Phil. Well, I declar! Done gone to Philadelphy—dis read de res' of dat letter, please sah.

Clarence. [*Reading.*]   "Deah old Phil: I does feel so entirely lonesome since I done leff you, in de city which you now is at."

Phil. Bless de dear lamb! dis listen at dat—he—he -aunty always did think a heap sight of ole Phil.   Dis please read dat over again.

Clarence. [*Reading.*]   "Deah old Phil: I does feel so entirely lonesome since I done leff you, in de city which you now is at."

Phil. [*Loud laughter.*]   Ha, ha, ha! he, he, he! I declar it makes me feel good clar down to my boots.

Clarence. [*Reading.*]   " Wouldn't you like to see aunty, and 'brace her wid dem dear arms once mo'? "

Phil. Did she say dat, for sure? Law bless you honey! I'd broke my two arms off.

Clarence. [*Reading.*]   " I does'nt like Philadelphy, cause I cant see de white of dem dear eyes of yorn."

Phil. Goodness to goodness! Aint dat sugar on hoe cake? yam—yam—umph !

Clarence. [*Reading.*]   " Well, dear Phil, dis is all at present; I will wind up dis 'pistle by sayin, de roses am red, de violets am blue, sugar am sweet, and so am you. From your ole friend, Aunt Judy Clemens, 301 Clay avenue."

Phil. Bless de dear soul, I'll done write to her dis night. I is very much 'bliged to you, sah.   What mout your name be?

Clarence. It is—oh, never mind that—but, my friend, I would like to ask a favor of you.

Phil. Yes, sah.

Clarence. I want to see your mistress.

Phil. [*Starting with surprise.*]   Oh, sah! I dont think she can see you.

Clarence. Can't you arrange it with her to see me out here?

Phil. No, indeed! you—you is't crazy is you? De house am full of company, and Miss Sibelle dont see anybody but quality folks.

Clarence. Ah! I thought her very charitable.

Phil. Oh, yes, she is, if you is beggin', she will see you.

Clarence. Begging! [*shakes his head.*] No, I am no beggar. God forbid I should beg from her.

Phil. I dont reckon you wants to find de company, does you?

Clarence. No, no. Do you think she would see me if I had news from Mr. Summerfield?

Phil. Dat Massa Summerfield dat used to be 'bout here?

Clarence. Yes; he sends her a message.

Phil. I dunno, I'll tell her, she mout see you, will you be here?

Clarence. I will conceal myself until she is ready to see me.

Phil. May be some time, but I t' ink she will see you.

Clarence. Tell me, who is her favorite now, among the gentlemen? Does Mr. Watson call, as usual?

Phil. Oh, yes, sah; he is here most of de time.

Clarence. Do you think she loves him?

Phil. Dunno, sah; 'pears mighty like it. [*Starts to leave.*

Clarence. Stay one moment, my good man! Does she ever mention Mr. Summerfield's name?

Phil. No, sah; she dont mention no man's name 'cept Massa Eugene Watson's.

Clarence. That is all. [*Exit* PHIL, L.] Then she loves him! Oh, how can I endure this? [*Exit* R.

Enter EUGENE WATSON, *from house.*

Eugene. Well, my scheme has worked admirably so far. In one short year, Clarence Summerfield has become a "total wreck." With the aid of liquor, faro bank, cards, and my well laid plans, I have succeeded in reducing him to poverty. But I will not stop until the grave closes over him; for should Sibelle learn of his whereabouts, she might induce him to reform. He loves her and might frustrate my plans. She must be mine at all hazards.

Enter COLLINS, R.

Collins. Good evening, Mr. Watson?

Eugene. Ah! good evening, Mr. Collins?

Collins. This is a delightful evening; the air is so bracing; something like the breeze on the beach—so refreshing—I tell you I enjoy the seashore, oh, it is fine—fine!

Eugene. Yes, it is very pleasant; I am rather partial to the seashore myself. City life becomes monotonous, especially in the sultry days of August, it is dreadful! Nothing like a small select party of jovial young people at a watering place. Not too large a party, but just a few ladies and gentlemen.

Collins. By the way, which are you going to this season: Saratoga, Newport, Atlantic City, or Cape May?

Eugene. I dont know. I thought of going to the White Mountains. I have some friends going there, and I think I would enjoy it better than at any other place.

Collins. The last time I was at the mountains I met Miss Sibelle and Mr. Summerfield. She looked lovely, handsome, beautiful! I believe she was considered the belle of the season. That was before she and Clarence had their little misunderstanding, you know.

Eugene. Oh, yes, I know.

Collins. I forgot. You know more about it than I. Too

bad to interfere with his love affairs, Eugene. Do you know
that he fell into the habit of drinking, on account of it?

Eugene. Why, no ; did he?

Collins. I should say he did. I saw him the other day, I
could hardly believe my eyes.

Eugene. Why so?

Collins. Well, sir, he was the most wretched looking being
I ever saw. I dont suppose, if you look the city over, you
could find a more pitiful sight.

Eugene. Why, you surprise me! Mr. Summerfield, the
wealthy young man, being reduced in so *short* a time!

Collins. Very singular, but true. It would not surprise me
if he were in the poor house by this time.

Eugene. Poor fellow!

Collins. Does Sibelle know it?

Eugene. I dont know ; if she does not, I think it better not
to inform her. It might make her unhappy. You know
she has a melancholly dispostiion.

Collins. Yes, I know. I wonder what is the cause of this
depression of spirit.

Eugene. I think she must have some deep sorrow, that is
working on her mind.

Collins. Very likely ; well, I must go in. Will you come?

Eugene. No : I'll promenade a while yet.

[*Exit* COLLINS *in house.*

Enter BOBY BURT, *by walk,* R. U. E.

Boby. Well, pard, I've been looking for you.

Eugene. And you are just the man I want to see. I have
got a little job I want worked up.

Boby. Say, cull, do I stand in with it?

Eugene. Yes, but we must talk fast, for you must not be
seen here. Summerfield is lurking around here; we must
get him out of the way. ·

· *Boby.* But I dont see any stamps in that.

Eugene. Once, when he was drunk, he deposited fifty
thousand dollars in a certain bank. Get him out of the way,
and the money will be ours.

Boby. You bet all your red chips on me. I am the boy
that can do that, and if I get copped I wont squeal.

Eugene. He is in love with Sibelle; tell him she is to be
married to-night.

Boby. What! you going to marry her?

Eugene. No, but tell him so ; induce him to fire the house
for revenge, he will go to prison, and we will claim the
money. If that fail, I have a bottle of drugged whiskey,
which will make him delirious. A small sum of money will
procure a certificate from a physician that will send him to
the insane asylum. Understand? crazy. I'll procure an

ambulance, and instead of sending him to the hospital, he
will go to the asylum. And if all fail, [*whispering in Boby's
ear*,] murder.

Boby. I am afraid we will have to croke him.

Eugene. If you find him, come here and let me know, but •
keep dark.

Boby. All right; but how do you like my togs? [*Turning
around.*] Aint they stunning?

Eugene. They are rather loud, too flashy—bad taste, bad
taste. But when did you make a raise?

Boby. I made a winning last night; a guy staked me, I
put my money down on the tray, it won through twice; then
I coppered the ten and played the king open, it came ten,
king, I won. So I came away with a big roll.

Eugene. You were quite lucky.

Boby. [*Takes off hat.*] How do you like my cady?

Eugene. It is altogether *too light;* but go, some one is coming.   ·   [*Exit* BURT, R.

Enter company of LADIES *and* GENTLEMEN *from house.*—SIBELLE
joins EUGENE, *and advances front.*—*Remainder of company promenade off' by walk,* R.

Eugene. Sibelie, this is no school boy's idle dream, it is love,
deep and devotional.

Sibelle. What is love, Eugene?

Eugene. Love is the reflection of God in man; no wrong
motive is actuated by love, and when passion rules the hour,
love takes its flight.

Sibelle. Does love die?

Eugene. Love dies with the soul.

Sibelle. Then love never dies?

Eugene. Love never dies.

Sibelle. Too true—I'll doubt no more.

Eugene. Yes, Sibelle, ours will be a path strewn with flowers of the sweetest fragrance. Our grounds adorned with a
silvery lake, where snow-white swans with silver-tipped
wings, will lightly skim o'er its smooth surface, while the
rippling waves silently kiss the pearly shore. Statuary of
unsurpassed beauty, promiscuously scattered o'er our gar-
dens. The gushing fountains will sparkle in the summer
sun, like myriads of diamonds, and the gold fish will sport
among the coral beds in the translucent water. The white
foam of the cascades will dance o'er crystalline rocks. Deer
will gambol on the verdant lawn, and play hide and seek
among the grottoes. Birds of different plumage will flap
their varigated wings in the exhilarating air, wafting to our
souls the sweet perfume. Golden-winged canaries, in silver
cages, will warble a sweet continual chorus. The rarest
paintings adorn our palace, and all else that art can add to
the transcendant beauty of our paradise on earth will be

ours. And when night takes the place of day, and the silent
stars their vigils keep, and the tinted lilies bathe in the dew
of heaven, our dreams will be of each other. Then, in the
sleep of death, where dreams are not, in love we'll live in
eternal bliss.

Sibelle. It is music sweet, at eventide, to hear the whip-poor-
will, that is nightly perched on yonder bow, and trills the
hours away, while its soft notes lull me to sweet forgetful-
ness; but sweeter still are thy noble sentiments of love.
[*Music within.*]   Play on, sweet music, play; penetrate the
inmost depth of my soul, and melt it in a mood to love.

Enter JOHN, *English footman, in livery.*

John. Ma'm, the carriage is waiting, hand the coachman
says as 'ow you 'ad better 'urry up, as the 'osses har getting
fretful!

Sibelle. I'll be there soon, John.

Enter COMPANY *from garden,* R. U. E., *and enter house, except*
MISSES JEWETT *and* MUNGER.

Sibelle. [*To Company.*]   Well, I must leave you for a short
time.

Miss Munger. Where are you going?   Not going to leave
us, are you?

Sibelle. Only for a short time, and I hope you will pardon
the breach of etiquette, in leaving you to entertain yourselves.

Miss Munger. Certainly; but this must be urgent business
that takes you away from such a gay company as has assem-
bled here to night.

Sibelle. Yes; I have heard, this evening, of a poor woman
in distress; she has three little children, and they are all in
destitute circumstances. I could not close my eyes in sleep
to-night, did I not go and see to their comfort. While we
have plenty, and are living in luxury, and even while, to
sweet music, we whirl in the mazy dance, we should remember the thousands that are suffering around us; and on such
occasions, should an opportunity offer itself, to relieve suffering humanity, it is our first duty to lay aside pleasure, and
go where charity calls.

Miss Jewett. Perhaps the cause of so much interest is due
to the fact that the sufferer is a woman?

Sibelle. No, Miss Jewett; where duty calls, there we should
go, be it man or woman; neither should we be predjudiced
against any nationality. America welcomes all to her free
shores, and it is the duty of every true American woman, to
extend *charity to all.*

Miss Jewett. Yes, Sibelle, we will excuse you; your efforts
in the way of doing good, will be rewarded. Go to the poor
woman, and may the blessing of heaven be with you!

[*Exit* MISSES JEWETT *and* MUNGER, *in house.*

Sibelle. Now, Eugene, good bye! I'll return soon; please make an apology to the guests for my absence.

Eugene. Yes, Sibelle; good bye, sweet!   [*They kiss.*

[*Exit* SIBELLE, *by walk,* R. U. E.

Enter EDA L. *and retires* L.

Eugene. How beautiful she looks to-night!—Now to get Summerfield out of the way; then I'll have his money, and Sibelle too. I'll go in and join in a quadrille, and perhaps when I'm through, Boby Burt will be somewhere about the premises.

Enter EDA THORNTON, *from house.*

Eda. Where have you been, all the evening, Eugene? I have been hunting you. Just think, you haven' danced with me to-night.

Eugene. Well, I declare, it is too bad; but then I have been bothered some with a head ache to-night, and I thought the night air might relieve me some; but I was coming in just as you came out.

Eda. And I just came out just as you were coming in. Eugene, are you sure your head aches? Hasn't there been some one out here that has attracted your attention? [*knowingly.*]

Eugene. My attention? why no, of course not; what makes you think so?

Eda. [*Slowly.*] Oh, I dont know—havent you been talking to any one—to somebody?

Eugene. No, no—let me see—no, I haven't spoken to any one out here to-night, except my friend Mr Collins.

Eda. I say, Eugene, does Mr. Collins wear dresses?

Eugene. Of course he dont wear dresses.   [*Uneasy.*

Eda. Did you kiss Mr. Collins, Eugene?

Eugene. No, I didn't kiss him—what do you mean?

Eda. Oh, nothing, I thought you kissed him; if you didn't kiss him it is all right, but I was beginning to feel *very* jealous.

Engene. Oh, you were? Well, let us go in now and have a waltz?

Eda. [*Meaningly.*] Eugene, dont you think it is *very* pleasant out here?

Eugene. [*Not understanding.*] Yes, it is pleasant, but I have been out all the evening.

Eda. I think is *awful* pleasant! Dont you like to be alone *sometimes*, when you have some one to talk to that you like very well?

Eugene. Oh, yes, I see [*kisses her*]; but let us go in and we can come out after awhile?

Eda. Well, just as you say.   [*Exit in house*

Enter BOBY BURT, R.

Boby. I dont see anything of Summerfield. I am afraid

I will have to give it up as a bad job. Ah! I wonder who that is coming?

Enter Mr. Partington, *as a Swell.*

Partington. Ah, gwacious, whose wesidence is this, Mistaw?

Boby. I give it up, ask me a harder one. [*Aside.*] I wonder if I couldn't cap him into a game.

Part. Ah, ah—you give it up ; yeas, yeas. I was stwolling awound, and thought I would come and see what was going on ; yeas, yeas.

Boby. They're having a high old time in there, some one going to be spliced.

Part. Ah, weally, I dont understand you. Spwiced ! spwiced—I dont understand.

Boby. I mean, some one going to get hitched.

Part. Ah, yeas, yeas—but Mistaw, will you please explain what you mean by hitched ?

Boby. Why some one going to be married.

Part. Ah, ah ! yeas, yeas, I understwand you now, I weally do. Who compose the happy pwair ?

Boby. I dont know ; some of the high-toned. Say, are you fond of sport?

Part. Varwy fond of spwort.

Boby. Well, come with me, I will show you a nice game.

Part. Is it a dewightful game ?

Boby. You'll think its delightful, if you ever go against it.

Part. Ah—yeas, yeas.   [*Exit* R., *arm in arm.*

Enter Phil, *from house.*

Phil. [*Looking out at walk.*] I wonder why Miss Sibelle dont come back ; she done gone some time now ! Dey wants her in de house to help 'range for de concert dat dey is gwine to have, for de benefit of de orphans' house, or someting else. Miss Sibelle has *more doins* and *carrings on* 'bout de poor white trash den I ever saw; now if she was fussing 'bout quality folks, dat would be different. Dey just keep ole Phil jumpin' round all de time—yes dey do. Been tryin' all de even' to get dat footman to write to Aunt Judy Clemens, but dey done took him away wid de carriage. I declar, if dar dont come dat rag man agin.

Enter Clarence, R. U. E., *walk.*

Clarence. Say, man, did you tell your mistress I wanted to see her?

Phil. No, sah ; Miss Sibelle done gone out.

Clarence. With whom did she go?

Phil. I dunno, sah ; I speck wid Massa Watson.

Clarence. Oh, curse that man—curse him—curse him !

Phil. [*Leaving hurriedly.*] Dat man is bad medicine, sho'. He's pizen, I'm a tellin' you !   [*Exit* Phil, *in house.*

Enter BOBY BURT, R.

Boby. My friend, you seem to be in distress, can I help you?

Clarence. No, I believe not; I am nearly past all help. You called me friend; I have no friends.

Boby. Then those that were your friends have deserted you; they have wronged, they have injured you.

Clarence. Yes, yes; so they have.

Boby. Even the lady, in whom you had so much confidence, was deceiving you. The lady who feigned friendship, the lady you loved, scorns you, while she is happy in the love of another.

Clarence. [*Sadly.*] Yes, I know it too well; I know it, but why add to my misery?

Boby. Believe me, I am your friend; I sympathize with you, and am sorry to see you in such a state of wretchedness, but, if I were you, while there was a spark of life left me to raise my hand against my offenders, I would be revenged.

Clarence. [*Angrily.*] So I will! what would you have me do? name it!

Boby. When all are asleep, to-night, fire the house and consume her to ashes. Will you do it?

Clarence. [*Emphatically.*] I will—I'll do it!

Boby. On your word and honor as a man?

Clarence. [*Thinking.*] No, no, friend, I can't do that; anything but that.

Boby. Do you know the cause of so much gayety here to-night?

Clarence. No, I do not; what is it?

Boby. Sibelle and Mr Watson are to be married to-night.

Clarence. [*Astonished.*] What is that I hear? Sibelle to be married! Oh, no, no—It must not be. Oh! why come here to taunt me? Leave me, man, leave me!

Enter EUGENE WATSON, R.

Boby. [*Aside to Eugene.*] Say pard, I weaken, he is game.

[EUGENE *gives* BURT *a reproachful look.*

Eugene. [*Advancing to* CLARENCE.] Ah, Clarence! how do you do?

Clarence. Sir, I dont shake hands with such as you.

Eugene. Why, what is the trouble?

Clarence. Trouble? trouble enough—dont ask me.

Eugene. Clarence, I am very much grieved to see you in this condition; but I will not wrong you by heaping blame upon you; for we are all liable to fall; we all; *all* have our faults.

Clarence. Yes, and *some* have more faults than others.

Eugene. Sir, do you wish to insinuate?

Clarence. If you consider it an insinuation, you can take it as such.

Eugene. Do you wish to insult me?

Clarence. I dont think I could *insult* you.

Eugene. Sir, I will not quarrel with you, you are beneath my notice.

[*Starting to leave, towards door steps,* CLARENCE *levels a pistol on him :* BOBY BURT *leaves stage hurriedly, with both hands on his ears.*]

Clarence. Eugene Watson! Put one foot on those steps and you are a dead man ; quit the premises immediately. [EUGENE *looks at* CLARENCE *a moment, and then starts to leave.*] but stay ; a few words.   [EUGENE *returns.*

Clarence. This weapon will be the means of launching my soul into eternity. Before I go, I will forgive you the wrong you have done me. Have you any whiskey to quench this dreadful thirst?

Eugene. Yes. I have some in my pocket ; here it is.

Clarence. [*Drinks and returns bottle.*] Sibelle has gone out; will she be back soon?

Eugene. I think she will—but you would not injure her?

Clarence. No, no—I would see her face once more, and then—farewell, until we meet in heaven. Oh! how my brain whirls around—all is growing dark—ah! ah!—

[*He falls;* EUGENE *looks over him.*

Eugene. The drug has done its work—he'll be raving bye and bye. [*A thought strikes him.*] I will kill him with Burt's knife [*produces knife*], and make my escape. His name is engraved on it, that will clear me. Sibelle's wealth, and fifty thousand dollars besides. [*Looking to see if any one is around.*] What, Sibelle coming! Curse the luck!

Enter SIBELLE, *by walk,* R.

Eugene. [*Extending hands.*] You have come. I have been waiting for you.

Sibelle. Have you? But what have you here?

Eugene. Sibelle, that is a crazy man that has wandered in here. Poor fellow!

Sibelle. Poor man, how wretched!

Eugene. I think it better to send for an ambulance, and have him taken to the hospital.

Sibelle. The insane asylum is the proper place to send him. Are you sure he is crazy?

Eugene. Yes ; quite sure.

Sibelle. Why couldn't we take him in the house until morning, he may only be intoxicated.

Eugene. Surely, you would not think of that. What would the guests say?

Sibelle. Guests? what do I care for guests when a suffering human being needs assistance? But, since *you* desire it, send for an ambulance.

Eugene. Yes; I'll go at once.   [*Exit*, EUGENE.

Clarence. [*Revives, looks wildly around.*] Oh, give me some whiskey—whiskey—whiskey.

Sibelle. Poor man, I see he is only intoxicated; he has been drinking. Yes, I'll take him in my house, and perhaps I can induce him to reform. He may be a man of noble principles, and can yet be saved from the mire into which he has fallen, and become a just and honorable man, a kind and affectionate father; a fond and loving husband and an ornament to society.

Clarence. [*Raising on elbow.*] Oh, could I see her face. Sibelle— Sibelle!

Sibelle. What is that I hear?—my name!—can it be he?

Clarence. That's it—that's it—"Beautiful Snow"—that is what she read to me. "Once I was pure as the beautiful snow."—If I could get some whiskey. I would not think of her.   [*Lays insensible.*

Sibelle. Yes, it is he—it is, it is. [*Arms around his neck and holds up his head.*] Clarence, speak to me! speak! Speak, Clarence, speak! [*With extreme emotion.*] What have I done to deserve this punishment? What have I done?
                                          [*She bends over him.*
END OF ACT II.   [*Curtain.*

ACT III.

SCENE. *Same as Act I.*—*Scene 1st; stand and checkers* R.; *stand and chess board*, L.; SIBELLE *and* EUGENE, R., CLARENCE *and* EDA, L., *playing. Curtain rises. They play silently.* CLARENCE *pays no attention to the game, but watches* SIBELLE, *jealously.*

Eda. Well, Clarence, why dont you move? I declare, you hardly know what you are doing!

Clarence. Is it my move? I thought it was yours.

Eda. You did, well you see you were mistaken.

Clarence. [*Moving and watching* SIBELLE. EDA *moves.*]

Eda. What is the matter, Clarence, have you lost your mind, why dont you move?

Clarence. [*Starting.*] Oh, yes, is it my move, where did you move?

Eda. I moved there [*pointing*], why dont you watch the game? I will surely get angry and quit the game if you continue so disinterested.   [*Moving.*

Eugene. There, Sibelle, I beat you, [*tapping her under the chin,*] didn't I?

Sibelle. Ah, that is too bad; but I'll play you another game.

Eda. Move, Clarence, move; you are not paying the least attention. What are you frowning at? [CLARENCE *pays no attention.*] There, now, I'm mad; I wont play any more.   [*Rising.*

Clarence. What did you say?—you were saying something just now, were you not? [EDA *looks provoked, and leaves room.* [CLARENCE *goes and sits at piano, fingering keys.*

Sibelle. There, Mr. Eugene, that makes two games I have beaten you, so you see you can't play as well as you thought you could. It may do you good to take some of that conceit out of you [*laughing*], ha, ha ha!

Eugene. Let us quit, I can't play any more; that ding donging on the piano makes me nervous; it bothers me.

Sibelle. Well, since you have lost interest in the game, we might as well quit.

Eugene. Just as you say, Sibelle; for anything you say is all right.

Sibelle. Ah!   [*Exit* SIBELLE, R. D.

Eugene. Clarence, do you play?

Clarence. No, I dont play; my playing bothers you; it makes you nervous. I may *sometime* have occasion to make you *more* nervous.   [*Exit* D. *in* F.

Eugene. Why! the man is angry at me; I thought we were friends.

Enter EDA, D. F.

Eda. Eugene, did you find Sibelle very interesting?

Eugene. Now, Eda, dont be foolish, you know we were only having a little game.

Eda. From what I saw, I thought you were having a pretty big game.

Eugene. Now, Eda, I did not think that of you; I did not think you would become jealous at nothing; we will not quarrel. Sing me one of your songs, will you?   [*Putting arm around her.*

Eda. Excuse me, Eugene, I don't feel like singing; I feel more like crying.

Eugene. Then I will not ask you; but you are looking very beautiful, to-day.

Sibelle. [*Walking in.*] Yes, she does look very beautiful to-day.   [EUGENE *starts,* SIBELLE *gives him a sharp look.*

Eda. Thanks, Sibelle.

Eugene. Yes, I mean—she is—she is—looking better than —than she used to look.

Sibelle. [*A look of reproach.*] Yes, she does indeed; I think the atmosphere agrees with her.

Eugene. Well, ladies, I have some business out in the city, which will take me away from you for a short time.

Sibelle. Wait, and I will order the carriage.

Eugene. Oh, no, it is not necessary, I can take a car.

Sibelle. I insist. [*Rings bell, enter* PHILIP.] Philip, the carriage!

Phil. Yes, marm; de carriage jis done driv around.

Eda. If you are going down Broadway, I will accompany you, as I have a little shopping to do, and you are going in the carriage.

Eugene. Certainly, Eda.

Eda. We will return soon, Sibelle.

[*Exit* EDA *and* EUGENE, D. F.

Sibelle. That woman is forever interfering with my plans. On account of Clarence I must stand by and witness Eugene's attentions to her and am forced to say nothing. How I hate her! I sometimes think Eugene does not care for me, but when we are alone, in each other's company, he is so kind and pleasant. Oh, I wish I knew! If any one should tell me he did not care for me I would not believe it. He says he must be polite to her, but I can see a little more than politeness; even now she is with him. Oh, I *must* tell Clarence that I am his sister. If I do not, it will drive me mad! but then I cannot marry Eugene—I did not think of that. Oh, this dreadful secret— must the dark clouds ever hang o'er me—will the sunshine never come? [*Rings bell, enter* PHILIP.] Philip, take that picture out of my room. Those cold hard features looking down at me, makes a chill run through my veins; and to think of his mysterious death makes my blood curdle. [*Hands over face.*] Ugh!

[PHIL *starts with fright, and looks behind him.*

Phil. Dont say dat, Miss Sibelle—I am not scared—it makes me feel kinder uncomfortable. Whar will I take it?

Sibelle. Anywhere, out of my sight—anywhere; in the garret.

[PHIL *looks frightened, scratches his head, and looks at* SIBELLE.

Phil. Does you mean me, Miss Sibelle?

Sibelle. Yes, Philip; take it in that dark gloomy garret, that is the proper place for it.

Phil. [*Shaking with fright.*] Oh, lor! can't you send Sarah up dar?

Sibelle. No; Sarah will not do.

Phil. All right. [*Aside.*] Ole Phil will never reach dat garret. [*Exit* PHIL, L. 1 E.

[SIBELLE *takes book at center table.*

Enter CLARENCE, D. in F.

Clarence. I have been out walking, Sibelle, who do you think I saw?

Sibelle. Oh, I don't know. I am not good at guessing who did you see, Clarence?

Clarence. Eda and Eugene strolling over the garden; they enjoy themselves very much; they enjoy each others society [SIBELLE *bites her lips*]. In fact, an observer would single them out as lovers: they remind me of two doves, and when I last saw them they were in the arbor, their favorite trysting place.

Sibelle. Are you sure, Clarence? They left in the carriage nearly an hour ago.

Clarence. They sent the carriage back ; Eugene, thinking the matter over, came to the conclusion that his business in the city was not of so much importance as he first thought. Oh, Sibelle, have you yet to learn the means lovers employ to effect a meeting? You know the old saying, " Lovers laugh at locksmiths."

Sibelle. Clarence, why did you tell me this?

Clarence. Oh, you are interested—I forgot!

Sibelle. No, no—but then—

Clarence. But what?

Sibelle. [*Half angrily.*] Nothing.

Enter PHILIP, D. *in* F.

Phil. 'Pears like its gwine to rain, Miss Sibelle, Mistah Eugene and Miss Eda'll get wet down dar, playing croquet.

Sibelle. [*Very angrily.*] Leave the room, sir !

Phil. Yes, marm.   [*Exit hurriedly*, D. *in* F.

Clarence. Didn't I tell you ?

Sibelle. I don't care, it is nothing to me.

[*Throws down book, provokingly.*

Clarence. Oh, I see you don't care, its somebody else, its nothing to you, oh, no; ha, ha, ha !

Sibelle. Well, I don't; there.   [*Turns her head and smiles.*

Enter EUGENE *and* EDA, D. *in* F.

Eda. We have had such a pleasant time playing croquet ; but it looked so much like rain, we were forced to come in.

Sibelle. I thought you were going out shopping.

Eugene. As it was late, and I could not see my man, I thought I would defer the call until a more favorable opportunity presented itself, and so Eda and I passed the time in a social game of croquet ?

Clarence. [*Seated at piano.*] What kind of croquet were you playing?

Eugene. Why, the usual game, of course.

Eda. I did not know of only one kind of croquet.

Clarence. Eda, did you ever hear this song ?

[*Singing.*]   " With his arms around her waist ;
Was that croquet? was that croquet? "

Ha, ha, ha ! Oh, you are very innocent.

Eda. I don't know what you mean.

Eugene. Neither do I.

Clarence. Oh, I suppose not ; ha, ha, ha !

[*Exit* CLARENCE, D. F.
[SIBELLE *gives* EUGENE *a withering look.*

Eda. Sibelle, it commenced to rain just as we reached the

house; but I think it is only a sun shower; we need rain so much; wont it make your flowers look nice, though!

Sibelle. [*Pleasantly.*] Yes, it will [*Exit* EDA.

Eugene. How have *you* been enjoying yourself, Sibelle?

Sibelle. I don't know as that would interest you if I should tell you. Eda seems to have wonderful powers of fascination; she has superior charms that more than satisfies you; she monopolizes your attention, while I am left to amuse myself the best I know how.

Eugene. Sibelle, you must not talk that way; you know I care for you and you alone.

Sibelle. You don't show it very much. Don't you suppose I can see? Don't you suppose I know? [*Angrily.*] What were you and Eda doing in the arbor, while you were out?

Eugene. [*Looking guilty.*] Who said we were in the arbor?

Sibelle. Oh, you need not plead innocent. I know, and I will not bear with your behavior any longer; and unless you cease your attentions to that *woman*, you can consider this our last interview. *I will not* bear with it any longer.

Eugene. I will not pay any more attention to her than politeness will admit.

Sibelle. [*Quickly.*] You must not even be polite to her—you love the woman—you can't fool me, Eugene. Yes; you love her and I hate her!

Eugene. I promise you Sibelle, I will only speak to her when I am obliged to.

Sibelle. You must not speak to her—do you understand that? [EUGENE *bites his lips with rage.*

Eugene. I understand.

Sibelle. Well, see that you do. [EUGENE *bows. Exit* SIBELLE.

Eugene. [*In a rage.*] Oh! she shall pay dearly for this humiliation. I am in her power *now;* but the time will come when she will be in mine, bowed at my feet. [*Exit* D. *in* F.

Enter PHIL., L. 1 E.

Phil. Dar, now, he is got his foot in it; he mought knowed better dan to be sparkin 'round Miss Eda, [*gathering up chess and checkers,*] kase when Miss Sibelle is mad she is bad, I tell you. Dey is some company in de parlor, I speck dey is gwine to come in heah in a minute, so I'll jis take dese out.

Enter PARTINGTON.

My golly, what a purty man! Goodness! dat's de purtiest man in New York.

Partington. Where is your mistwess?

Phil. [*Looking at him.*] Ha, ha, ha! His mouf looks puckered up, like he'd been eatin' green persimmons.

Partington. What were you wemarking?

Phil. Dis lessen at dat. Does you mean Miss Sibelle?

Partington. Ah! yeas, yeas.

Phil. Say, boss, you aint well, is you? What is you been
eatin?
Partington. Oh, this is howid.
Phil. Miss Sibelle be heah after while. I reckon.
                                          [*Exit* PHIL, R. D.
Partington. Yeas, yeas; I will wait.

Enter SIBELLE, R. D., PARTINGTON *bows very low.*

Partington. Ah! Miss Sibelle, I believe. [SIBELLE *bows.*]
I called to see Mr. Watson; I was infwormed that he was
wisiting heah; I would like to see him on impwortant business. My name is Partington.
Sibelle. I will find him.   [*Exit* D. *in* F.
Partington. Ah, thanks! What a charmwing cweture;
perhaps she would not object to my attentions. I will twy
her.

Enter SIBELLE *and* EUGENE; SIBELLE *introduces* PARTINGTON *to*
EUGENE; *both gentlemen bow and shake hands.*

Partington. I was infwormed that you were wisiting heah.
I wanted some infwamation concerning a most deswirable
wesidence that you have for sale. I called at your employ-
ah's office and he was not in. Are you doing much in weal
estate, Mr. Watson?
Eugene. Yes, very well; but in regard to that residence,
I dont know anything about it. Mr. Worthington just en-
tered it on his books this morning.

Enter MR. COLLINS *and* MISS JEWETT, D. *in* F.

Partington. Ah! yeas; well I can see you again.
Eugene. Yes, yes.
    [EUGENE *bows to* MISS JEWETT *and* MR. COLLINS. SI-
    BELLE *introduces them to* PARTINGTON. PARTINGTON
    bows very low.
Partington. Miss Sibelle, you have a verwy fine location
here, I admwire it very much; the gwounds are beautifully
laid out, and such exquisite flowahs—delightful flowahs.
Sibelle. Yes; it is quite pleasant.

Enter MISS MUNGER, MR. ALLEN, EDA *and* CLARENCE. SIBELLE
    introduces PARTINGTON. *All seated.*

Partington. Miss Sibelle, you have a gweat deal of compa-
ny; they can't wesist coming to this lovely we-tweat, espes-
cially when there is such an entertwaining young lady at the
head of the house.
Sibelle. Do you think so?
Partington. I weally do.
Sibelle. I thank you very much for the compliment, Mr.—
Partington. Partington is my name; here is my card.
Gwacious! how stupid I am, not to give you my card be-

fwore. Now, if you can favor us with some music, I think it could not be otherwise than highly appweciated.

Sibelle. I am sorry to say I haven't given any attention to music for some years, so I hope you will excuse me.

Eugene. No. Mr. Partington; Sibelle devotes all of her spare time to the poor.

Partington. Yes; I thought she had an obliging disposition.

Sibelle. I am afraid you are addicted to flattery, Mr. Partington.

Partington. Ah. no; I weally speak the truth. I could not speak too highly of you.

Enter PHILIP, R. D., *with tray of wine; in passing it around he does not notice* PARTINGTON.

Phil. [*Aside.*] Dar's dat party man again.

Sibelle. [*After wine is passed, and* PHIL *sets tray on center table.*] Is this Conig or Heidsic, Philip?

Phil. [*Looking at* PARTINGTON.] Yes, marm; he looks sick.

Sibelle. [*Tasting wine.*] No, it is Conig.

Phil. [*To himself.*] His name is Conig; Mr. Conig.

Sibelle. Why, Mr. Partington, you have no Champagne. Philip, Mr. Partington. [*Meaning to hand him wine.*

Phil. [*Extending his hand.*] How de do, sah? I was under de 'pression dat your name was Mistah Conig.

Partington. Good gwacious, how absurd!

Sibelle. Philip, hand Mr. Partington some wine.

Phil. Yes, marm.

[*Hands him wine, and upsets it in* PARTINGTON'S *lap.*

Partington. [*Wiping himself with handkerchief.*] Good Gwacious! this is dwedful!

[PHIL *brushes him hastily with dust brush.*

Phil. Dar, sah, you is all right.

Sibelle. Philip, you are very stupid to-day. Mr. Partington, you have been rather unfortunate.

Partington. Yeas, yeas; extwemely unfortunate.

Phil. [*At center table.*] I is a good templar; I dar not drink dis wine—dog my buttons, if I believe it is wine. [*Tastes it.*] It's cidah— no 'taint cidah, it's Magnolia Balm, or Mrs. Winslow's Soothing Syrup, dat's what it is. [*Tastes again.*] No— no, sah, it's Florida water, sho' as you was born. [*Drinks a glass.*] I declar! dis tastes dis like tar juice.

Sibelle. Philip!

Phil. Yes, marm. [*Gathers up wine glasses and leaves room.*

Partington. I propose we have a quadrille.

Eda. Yes, a quadrille.

Partington. That will be chawming. [*After they all have chosen partners.*] Good gwacious! I am left. [*After quadrille.*] Miss Munger, if you are not too twiard, let us have a waltz.

Miss Munger. Certainly.

[*They waltz; all rest company join in.*

Phil. [*After waltz.*] Miss Sibelle, refreshments am ready.
[*Exit* PHIL.
Partington. Ah, wefeshments.   [*Exit all except* PARTINGTON.]
[*In natural voice.*] Well, I think my disguise as a swell is
complete. Eugene Watson is the man I am after; I must
make it convenient to call here often.

Enter SIBELLE, L. D.

Sibelle. All alone, Mr. Partington? Are you not going out
to refreshment?
Partington. Wefeshments?   Ah, yeas, yeas.
Sibelle. If Mr. Watson is not engaged, please say to him I
would like to see him.
Partington. Ah, yeas, yeas; he seems to be wonderfully in-
terwested in the lovely Miss Eda. When do you think will
be the eventful time? I mean the wedding.
Sibelle. I am sure I do not know; you will have to inquire
of some one more informed on the subject.
Partington. Ah, yeas, yeas.   [*Exit* PARTINGTON, L. D.
Sibelle. Oh, I cannot bear this longer ; their intimacy is becoming the general subject of conversation among my guests.

Enter EUGENE, L. D.

Eugene. All alone? why do you not join in the festivities?
You are not very gay of late.
Sibelle. From all appearances, and from what I hear, you
have been enjoying the festivities. I am not so charming or
interesting as some one else who favors you with her delight-
ful company.
Eugene. I did not expect this rebuke from you ; I thought
I would find you, and we would have a pleasant time.
Sibelle. Find me? Yes ; when I sent for you, you thought
it time to find me—and as for a pleasant time. I think our
pleasant times are past.
Eugene. I will leave you until you are in a better mood.
Exit D. *in* F.
Sibelle. He little knows the woman he is tampering with.

Enter CLARENCE, D. *in* F.

Clarence. Sibelle, I have some news, which, perhaps it
would be as well to tell you. It is this : after thinking the
matter over for some time, I have finally decided to leave
America.
Sibelle. Why this sudden freak ?
Clarence. From the first time I saw you there has been a
strange fascination that has ever drawn me toward you; you
have been kind—very kind at times, but it changed to cool
indifference. I bore it with an aching heart, still hoping to
win ; but I now see it is useless to hope on, and I am re-
solved to see you no more. Sibelle, I have long treasured
up the thought that I might one day fill a place in your

heart. My efforts have been in vain, and I cannot stand by and see you smile on another—to see you devote the most of your time to another—in fact, to know that you love him. Sibelle, I have come to bid you good bye; it will be a long time before we meet again; perhaps we may never meet again! Oh, what a sad, sad thought. And when the dark, green waves of the ocean roll between us, and I have no familliar scenes to look upon, save the bright sun and twinkling stars, in memory I will live o'er this scene, and those moments will be the most unhappy of my life. [*Takes her hand.*] Good bye, Sibelle, for the last time. Yes, the *last time*.

Sibelle. Then indeed, you *are* going! Oh, Clarence, could I only persuade you! You do not know how much I am interested in you. Could you believe me should I tell you all?

Clarence. After what has passed—after what I have seen, I do not think anything you could say would have any force.

Sibelle. Oh, Clarence, do not leave me subject to the intrusions of this unfeeling man.

Clarence. What! do you wish to taunt me further? Why do you recall that man? Ah, fair but false woman, it would be well not to tempt me to the extreme—you do not know me.

Sibelle. I mean what I say; I do not wish to be left with that unfeeling man.

Clarence. Oh, how deceitful! Your affected manners, your feigned fond affection, your double meaning words, your smooth oily tongue, your forced fascinating smile. Oh, I *hate* you!

Sibelle. I never thought such words would come from your lips; but then, I'll forgive you, bacause—

Clarence. Because what?

Sibelle. Because you are very dear to me.

Clarence. Oh, that I did know it!

Sibelle. You say I love another; then will you leave me with this man that causes you so much displeasure?

Clarence. Oh, vilest of the vile, I could sever that tongue from its roots. Oh, fool that I am! You shall pay for your base deception. [*Produces knife.*

Sibelle. [*Quickly.*] No, no, no—you would not murder me! Have mercy, do not murder me! Think how your mother would feel to know that you were a murderer! [*With great emotion.*] Oh, think that I am your si—

Clarence. My what!

Sibelle. Your Sibelle.

Clarence. Turn that false face from me; those eyes will make me break my resolve—that false face—a living lie that will hurl your soul into perdition, and fiends will snatch at it!

Sibelle. For heaven's sake. Clarence, do not murder me!
Clarence. Nothing can win me from my purpose. No, foul
wench—devil! you have ruined me with your wonderful in-
nocence. A lie—nothing but a lie; Satan has made you so;
he painted your cheeks and limned your smile, and every
delicate feature, that you might lure good men to death and
hell. He puts on such a pretty garb as yours, and counts
his worshipers by the score. I will see your false face no
more. You have made a demon of me, [*approaching her,*]
and when you feel the cold steel piercing your heart, know
that I have revenge!
          [*Clutches her around the neck, and raises the knife.*
Sibelle. [*Shrieking with alarm.*] Clarence, I am your sister.
      [CLARENCE *drops the knife in wonder and astonishment,
      and gazes vacantly at her.*
                                                    [*Curtain.*

                  END OF ACT III.

_____

                  A C T   I V .

SCENE. *Same as Scene* 1, *Act I.* SIBELLE *seated at table,* R. C. .

Sibelle. I am to give him an explanation; I tremble at the
thought. Oh, must I perform the dreadful task? Why did
Providence tear me away from home and friends—from all
that is near and dear to me. How long am I to endure this
fear—this burden? Oh, I cannot tell him that I, his sister,
have been tried for murder. He comes. Now, kind heaven,
aid me in this new trial.

                  Enter EUGENE, D. *in* F.

Sibelle. [*Aside.*] That detestable man! [*To* EUGENE.] What,
you here, Mr. Watson? I did not think you could have the
assurance to intrude upon my privacy, after what I gave you
to understand last evening. How dare you enter a lady's
apartment in this manner? Did I not forbid you coming in
my presence—at my house?
Eugene. I thought, perhaps, you might have occasion to
relent. I have come to make amends for the past, and I
hope you will be reconciled to what I have to say, and not
judge too hastily. If I have, by word or action ever given
you offense, I am very sorry indeed. Or, if this estrange-
ment is due to the fact of my attention to Eda, I will
simply say that I was not contemplating anything more
serious than friendship in regard to her; in fact, I can say I
do not even enjoy her company; but if that has raised any
serious objections in your mind, I pray you dispel them.

Anything I have said or done that has not been pleasant to you, I am willing to retract. I can assure you it was not my intention to give offense; but if you consider that I have, I humbly ask your pardon, and if, on due reflection, you can become my wife, I will be all to you that becomes a husband. Have you any answer?

Sibelle. Mr. Watson, this is mockery; I will not presume that you love me. You do not even care enough to respect me; your conduct has shown it. Do not think I do not understand you!

Eugene. Sibelle, I do not know what you mean.

Sibelle. I mean that you have forfeited all respect I once had for you. Your designs are of the basest character. Your deception is cloaked in smooth propositions, which are as hateful as they are insulting. You will confer a great favor on me by leaving my presence.

Eugene. Then you do not consent to be my wife?

Sibelle. Sir, it is useless to ask such questions. No, sir, *that* can never be; I would rather die than be *your* wife! I wish to be alone.

Eugene. Certainly, I will leave your presence; but I will call again. I have one more call to make on you, which I consider of great importance.

Sibelle. It cannot be of any importance to me, so you need not put yourself to any inconvenience—to speak more plainly, I will not permit you to call again.

Eugene. Good bye; I will call again; you may change your mind before many hours.

Sibelle. I will *never* change my mind.

Eugene. [*Throwing kiss at her.*] Ta, ta—good day, proud beauty. Tral- la—la! [*Exit,* D. *in* F.

Enter PARTINGTON, L. D.

Partington. Ah, good day, Miss Sibelle; I was out walking, and I thought I would stwop in a few moments; are you well?

Sibelle. [*Pleasantly.*] Yes, thank you; sit down.

Partington. Ah, yeas, yeas; you have a very deswirable wesidence; every one that passes makes some complimentary wemark. You should hear the exclamations: such as "beautiful," "handsome," "delightful surwoundings," "isn't it lovely?" "what exquisite flowahs!" I don't think you know how much it is apweciated.

Sibelle. I am much obliged for your compliments, Mr. Partington; but people sometimes over estimate, you know, and they are not any less extravagant in their remarks, especially when the object of their admiration is immediately connected with a lady. You know unjust praise is flattery.

Partington. Ah, yeas, yeas; but I do not think I have been extwavagant in my appweciation of your handsome wesi-

dence.   It weminds me of some of the dwellings down south.
Sibelle. You have traveled in the south? What part do
you have reference to?

Partington. Oh, most of the southern cities have wesi-
dences with verwy nice gwounds, shrubbery and flowahs,
and some of the plantwations are extwaordinary. By the
way, Mr. Watson has been in that country, I believe.

Sibelle. Yes, it is singular ; we had the pleasure of meeting
in Mobile some five years ago ; we went down on the beach
for a ride.   I remember the harness broke, and in trying to
mend it he cut his finger ; it bled freely ; I tied it up with
my handkerchief.   I think it caused him considerable pain.
When we met here, I did not recognize him until he recalled
the incident.

Partington. That is wather womantic.   As we must con-
wibute something for all of our pleasures, I suppose you lost
your handkerchief, glove or a bow of ribbon.   The ladies
invawibly lose some little thing ; you understand.

Sibelle. I dont remember whether I lost anything or rot ;
Mr. Watson left the city that night.   I don't remember
whether he gave me my handkerchief or not ; but then so
small a loss would be nothing.

Partington. Ah, no ; but if your name was on it, the finder
would have sent it to you, no doubt.

Sibelle. Yes, it had my name on it.

Partington. [*Aside.*] The *very* handkerchief! Ah, I almost
forgot.   I promwist to see Mr. Watson heah on some business, that was the weal cause of my stwopping.

Sibelle. [*Surprised.*] Did you?   I don't think he will come.

Partington: Why not? why not?

Sibelle. Oh—he—he may, if you have arranged on meeting
here.   If that is the case, I will retire until your interview
is at an end.   [*Exit* R. D.

Partington. [*Natural tone of voice.*] There is something
wrong here.   What was that she said? [*Thinking.*] Oh, yes ;
" He may come, if you have arranged a meeting here."
Then he does not come here any more!   Why he talked as
if he were still the favorite ; I will wait and see if he comes.
If he should not, I must find him, and that to-day, too.   I
think I hear some one coming.

Enter EUGENE, D. *in* F.

Eugene. Ah, Mr. Partington, you are punctual.   I came
very near changing my mind, for reasons best known to myself ; but as you wished to see me, I thought I would not
disappoint you.   I was here a short time ago.

Partington. Ah, yeas, yeas ; I apweciate your kindness, I
weally do.   I believe I explained to you why I did not want
to see you at your office.

Eugene. Yes, you did ; that is all right ; and now I am prepared to furnish you with the information you desire concerning that real estate. I think you had better decide at once, as there are several parties very anxious to purchase; but in order to hold it, as I knew you wanted it, I told my employer that I thought I had a better bargain in you.

Partington. Ah, yeas, yeas; you were verwy kind to look after my interest, and you will allow me to thank you but as I have decided not to wemain in the city—

Eugene. Oh, I understand; you have your eye on some other city. Well, it doesn't make the least difference to us, as the property is ready sale. I thought you wanted it, that's all.

Partington. I did wish to purchase when we first talked on the subject, but I think I will take a trip over the southern country, and see what I can do there.

Eugene. Ah, now you interest me. What part of the south do you intend to go? I have been in that country a great many times, perhaps I could give you some information as to a good locality.

Partington. I did not know that you had been in the south, or I certwainly would have inquired before; but I think the fwirst cities I will wisit will be Charleston and Mobile; they tell me there are some handswome ladies in those two cities.

Eugene. I see, Mr. Partington, you are a great ladies' man, and I don't think there are many that could resist your winning address; ha, ha, ha!

Partington. Ah, now weally, Mr. Watson, I did not think you were addicted to flatterwy. Have you ever been in Mobile?

Eugene. Let me see. [*Thinking.*] It seems to me—no—no, I never was in Mobile, but I have been in most all the other cities.

Partington. I believe Miss Sibelle is from the south, is she not?

Eugene. Sibelle? I am sure I don't know: I never thought to inquire.

Partington. We were talking about the ladies—

Eugene. Yes; I found some handsome ladies, one in particular, in the city of Mo—[*confused,*] in the city of—it is strange I can't remember—Macon, that is the place.

Partington. One does *sometimes* forget; but how about the lady?

Eugene. Oh, nothing, a ride on the beach, that is all.

Partington. Is there a beach near Macon?

Eugene. Did I say beach? I meant in the country.

Partington. [*Aside.*] That is all I want to know. [*To* EUGENE.] Well, Mr. Watson, I have some business out in the city; I will see you again; good day.   [*Exit* D. *in* F.

Eugene. Good gracious! I came very near making a slip

of the tongue; I came very near saying •Mobile, the very
thing I did not want to say. I got out of it very well; that
silly fool will not understand. I don't believe he knows a
"deswirable wesidence," as he calls it, when he sees one. I
think I am safe, after five years away. [*Listening.*] I think
I hear Sibelle coming: I will tell her I know her secret—she
must be my wife—*that* plan cannot fail, if all else should.

Enter PHILIP, D. *in* F.

Eugene. Where is your mistress?
Phil. Dunno, sah; speck she is gone out somewhar, I seed
de carriage drive around. I speck she is done gone by dis
time.
Eugene. Perhaps she has. Tell her I called—you know—
Mr. Watson.
Phil. Yes, sah. [*Bowing.*]   [*Exit* WATSON, D. *in* F.

Enter SIBELLE, R. D.

Phil. Miss Sibelle, dat gemman, Mistah Watson, was heah,
and he axed me to say dat he called.   *Exit* PHIL.
Sibelle. Could he have the assurance to leave word to me?
Had I known, before last night, his true character, I would
have avoided him—such a cool, calculating man is to be
feared. Clarence will be here in a few minutes; he said he
wanted to know of my past life. Oh, what shall I tell him
in regard to my husband? I cannot tell him my secret; and
if I tell him my name, he may know something about it.
Oh, heavens! he is coming; what shall I do?

Enter CLARENCE, D. *in* F.

Clarence. Sister, what makes you always look so sad? have
you not found your brother? We ought, indeed, to be
happy. Sit down, and let us have a social chat.   [*They sit.*
Sibelle. [*Trying to look pleasant.*] Do I look sad, Clarence?
I think it only imagination on your part.
Clarence. Oh, no; it is not imagination; perhaps Mr. Watson
has something to do with your gloomy disposition. I sup-
pose you will marry him?
Sibelle. No, Clarence; I will never marry that man. I de-
spise him; he is no companion for a lady.
Clarence. Why, Sibelle, I thought you loved him. How
long have you been of this opinion?
Sibelle. Since last night; his true character was revealed
to me, and now I detest him.
Clarence. What do you mean? What did he say? Any-
thing to offend? Come, explain.
Sibelle. Clarence, do not ask me; you will know all in time.
[CLARENCE *thinking.*] What are you thinking about?
Clarence. I was thinking about your name; Nellie is your

name; why did you change it? Do you think Sibelle prettier than Nellie?

Sibelle. Nellie, Nellie? I do not—know Nellie? I do not understand—was it Nellie? [*Aside.*] Have I forgotten my own name? Can this be a mistake?

Clarence. [*Looking puzzled.*] Why, what is the matter? Don't you know when you left home your name was Nellie?

Sibelle. [*Confused.*] Yes yes—but—I mean—have you heard from mother lately?

Clarence. Yes; I have a letter here, just received. [*Produces letter.*] I will read it.

Sibelle. Yes, do. [*Aside.*] This cannot be my brother after all.

Clarence. [*Reading.*] "New Orleans, July 16th, 1878. My dear son, Clarence.

Sibelle. [*Aside.*] Clarence? *My brother's* name is Will. [*To* CLARENCE.] Does she live in New Orleans, now?

Clarence. Now? why of course, we always lived in New Orleans; don't you remember?

Sibelle. No; I do not remember. I thought we lived on a plantation.

Clarence. Well, when you left home you were so young it is very likely that you have forgotten.

Sibelle. Possibly; but go on with the letter.

Clarence. [*Reading.*] "After these many years, I have received a letter from our darling lost Nellie, that we thought dead."

Sibelle. [*Aside.*] No; this is not my brother.

Clarence. [*Reading.*] "Only think, the letter was over two months coming. She said, she and an old sailor were the only survivors of the wrecked vessel, in which she and her uncle sailed. That she lived with the old sailor's family, until quite a young lady, married a young man of industrious habits, who, in time, became wealthy."

Sibelle. [*Aside.*] How is this mistake? I do not understand.

Clarence. [*Reading.* "But died suddenly, with heart disease, [SIBELLE starts.] leaving his entire fortune to her. She also said she would come to America, and reside in New York, but would pay us a visit first. I received this letter over two years past. I answered it but have not heard from her. Perhaps she is now in New York. I am glad to know that your accident did not prove as serious as it was thought at first. Hoping you will be home soon, I am as ever, your affectionate mother." [*Folding letter.*] So, sister, you see how things have come around; and we will go home together, and give them an agreeable surprise.

Sibelle. Yes; but let me look at those photos again, will you Clarence?

Clarence. Certainly. [*Handing them to her. After a silence.*]
What are you looking at so long?

Sibelle. [*Holding up her mother's picture.*] Do you think it is
a good picture?

Clarence. Well, really, I don't know.

Sibelle. You don't know; who does?

Clarence. In fact, I never saw the lady; therefore, I could
not say. · It is a picture, I think, a detective left in my room,
who came to inquire into the particulars of my case. I think
he left a letter, too, by some mistake, perhaps dropped it on
the floor. The nurse must have put them with mine. You
will find the letter there. I think his name is Will Hastings.
But why do you ask?

Sibelle. Oh, I--I had some friends by that name, that is all.
[*Keeps her mother's picture, and* HASTING'S *letter, hands
rest back.*]

Clarence. I think you act very strangely; since you have
learned all about your family, you do not seem very much
pleased.

Sibelle. [*Pleasantly.*] Oh, yes, I am.

Clarence.] Had it not been for these letters, you would not
have found your brother, and perhaps we might have been
married.

Sibelle. As we did not know that we were brother and sister,
it would not have been very singular, as young people do
sometimes marry.

Clarence. Ah, now you are joking—ha, ha! Well, good bye
for the present, I am going out to take a little air.
                              [*Exit* D. *in* F.

Sibelle. Then this is not my brother. How singular my
brother's letter should fall into my hands—a detective too—
why did I not think to read his letter? I would, if I had
thought Clarence was not my brother. Ah, my secret is
still safe; I did not tell him; why didn't I? How strange
this all is! Perhaps this Will Hastings is not my brother.
I will read his letter. [*Opens and reads.*] "Detective Will
Hastings: The Mrs. Saunders you are after, is the Sibelle
that I told you of; she resides in the city. You have the
number; she resembles her mother. W. R. C." Great
Heavens! a detective on my track, and he my brother!
Yes, my brother, for he had my mother's picture; but let
me see! [*Looks at letter.*] "She resembles her mother." Oh,
might he not have it to trace me up? Oh, what can this
mean? But stop, it is his name—it must be he. Oh! what
will I do if it is not?

                    Enter PARTINGTON, D. *in* F.

Partington. Ah, Sibelle, I have come to tell you some news;
and you must not be frightened when I tell you my name is
not Partington; but I am a detective. Your name before

marriage was Julia Hastings. I am your br ther, Will Hastings!

Sibelle. [*Aside.*] Oh. can it be he? [*Aloud.*] My brother?
[*Looks at him with suspicion and doubt.*
[*Curtain.*

END OF ACT IV.

ACT. V.

TIME. *Night.*
SCENE. *Same as Act IV.*

Enter PARTINGTON, D. *in* F. *Takes off hat and gloves. Natural tone of voice.*

Partington. Well, as Sibelle is not here, I will sit down until she comes. [*Sits* R., *reading paper.*

Enter PHILIP, D. *in* F.

Phil. Law sakes alive! . If dar airt dat fancy man again.
[*Bows to* PARTINGTON.] How de do sah?

Partington. Te'l your mistress I want to see her.

Phil. [*Aside.*] I declar! Dat man done changed his language—talks dis de same as people now. Dar is somfen wrong heah, sho', [*shakes his head.*] I'm a tellin' you!
[*Exit* PHIL, R. D.

Enter SIBELLE, R. D.

Sibelle. Good morning, brother! why didn't you stay here last night, as I requested? I have the nicest room for you; a perfect bijou. I think you will admire it.

Partington. No doubt, sister, it is very nice, and I would enjoy it very much; but I was compelled to be elsewhere. You know with a detective. business is business, and sometimes it is *not* the *most pleasant* occupation in the world.

Sibelle. At times it is not very pleasant, I should imagine. It must be a very queer business! You know, the first time you called here, I thought you a silly fool?

Partington. Yes, sometimes I have to play the fool; sometimes I play drunk, or most any way, just as it is required; I have to work myself into the first society, then in the lowest; I must be up early and late in club rooms and gambling houses; then, perhaps I am required to get some information from a minister; I frame some excuse to have an interview, and gain my object without him knowing my real business.

Sibelle. Why don't you quit this disagreeable mode of life?

Partington. Well, sister, my detective career is nearly at an end. I have only one object to accomplish, and then I will be happy.

Sibelle. Yes: you told me you were not employed by any one, and I would like to know what that object is.

Partington. Can you not guess?

Sibelle. No, not unless—is it concerning the mystery?

Partington. Yes; and I think I have found the guilty one. [SIBELLE *is startled with fright.*] What makes you look frightened?

Sibelle. Oh, sir, are you my brother? I fear I am being led into some trap to wring information from me.

Partington. Why, do I not know your secret?

Sibelle. [*Frightened.*] My secret! Oh, Heavens!—Do you—do you know it? Tell me—tell me! You do not.

Partington. Yes; have I not told you it?

Sibelle. Yes; but you—I—I—you—you are a detective.

Partington. You must not be frightened; I am your brother Will. Did I not show you your mother's picture?

Sibelle. Why don't you say, *our* mother's picture?

Partington. I mean our mother. Sister, I tell you truly, I am your brother.

Sibelle. How can you prove it? Oh, sir, prove it!

Partington. Can you remember, a long time ago, a beautiful white house, on the bank of a river?

Sibelle. [*Excited.*] Yes, yes; go on.

Partington. The beautiful flowers; the white rows of negro huts.

Sibelle. [*Clapping her hands.*] Yes, yes; but go on.

Partington. How we used to watch the steamboats going up the river; how we played under the willow trees, and sailed our little boats in the pond; how we played with the hounds, and rode on the loads of cotton.

Sibelle. Now I remember all. [*Joyfully.*] You are my brother. [*Embracing.*] You are my brother!

Partington. Yes, sister; then the dark hour came, when you were stolen away. It almost broke poor mother's heart. Oh, that was a sad time.

Sibelle. Poor mother! When did you hear from home?

Partington. Oh, not long since; but many changes have taken place since you left; many sad changes.

Sibelle. Tell me, Will, how is mother?

Partington. Oh, Julia, do not ask me.

Sibelle. Oh, tell me the worst!

Partington. Julia, mother is dead.

Sibelle. Dead? My poor mother! my poor mother! [*After a silence.*] And father?

Partington. Oh, Julia, he too is dead.

Sibelle. Father, too? all gone! [*Arm around his neck.*] No one left me but you, Will, you will be a friend to me, wont you, Will? I have no one on earth, but you—all are gone—all are gone!

Partington. Yes, Julia: I will be your friend as none but a brother can.

Sibelle. Yes, I know you will.

Partington. Julia, I came to-night to get some important information from you; but I do not feel like broaching the subject, in the present state of your feelings. I have not many minutes to spare, as I am obliged to leave for Boston.

Sibelle. If what you wish to know is important, it is my duty to tell you.

Partington. I will not ask you anything, only what I am obliged to. Do you remember the ride on the beach with Watson?

Sibelle. Yes.

Partington. Do you remember whether he gave back the handkerchief you tied around his hand? You know it was found in your husband's room the next morning.

Sibelle. [*Thinking.*] No, I do not remember.

Partington. That is of great importance to me. By the way, I have been under the impression that you were in love with Mr. Watson; in fact, I thought you would marry him.

Sibelle. What! marry Mr. Watson? I despise him. No, I will never marry him.

Partington. I am glad to hear it, for I have a little business with him, which he will not enjoy very much.

Sibelle. Lately I have thought him a villain.

Partington. That is all, now I must go; will you please lend me a handkerchief until I return from Boston?

Sibelle. Yes. [*Exit* SIBELLE, R. D.

Partington. She does not love him, and will not marry him; she is safe: I will let him go until my return.

Enter SIBELLE, R. D.

Sibelle. Will this one do?

Partington. Yes, thanks; what is this? Oh, I see, your name. [*Reads.*] "Mrs. Julia Saunders." Well, good bye! I think I will be back in two weeks.

[*They kiss. Exit* PARTINGTON, D. *in* F.

Sibelle. Oh, I am so sorry he is gone. I will be all alone, now, except when Clarence is here. I can't enjoy Eda's company. [*Exit* R. D.

Enter EUGENE *and* EDA, D. *in* F. *They sit at center table.*

Eda. You say you have proposed, and she has refused you. I cannot think of this dreadful plan without trembling, and I feel very thankful that it has terminated as it has; sometimes I think that you might love her—that you might be playing false to me—that once when married to her, I would be cast off. There is danger, for Sibelle is very beautiful.

Enter SIBELLE, D. *in* F., *unobserved.*

Eugene. Fear not. Eda; I really do not think Sibelle is beautiful. She is passable, that is all.

Eda. Are you sure you do not like her just a little bit?

Eugene. Why, Eda, of course not; but, you know, money we must have; then our nice little cottage at some watering place; or in the mountains; or at some other desirable place where we can live and enjoy each other's love in blissful quietude.

Eda. I will be so happy; but then she has refused you, how are you going to manage it?

Eugene. Oh, that is easy enough; I have other means more persuasive.

SIBELLE *walks front of them.*

Eugene. What, Sibelle?

Eda. [*Both rising.*] Good gracious!

Sibelle. [*Pointing finger to door in* F.] Eugene Watson and Eda Thornton, leave my house!

Eugene. But Miss—

Sibelle. Leave my house!   [*Exit* EDA, D. *in* F.

Eugene. I must explain; you do not understand.

Sibelle. I understand enough.

Eugene. No; you do not understand that you are to be my wife.

Sibelle. Insulting villain! How dare you talk in that manner?

Eugene. I dare do anything. [*Producing pistol.*] And now consent to be my wife, or I will see what this will do.

Sibelle. [*Coolly.*] Ah, then this is the more persuasive means. Sir! you do not know the woman you are dealing with. I care not for my life, take it—kill me, I will not be your wife. Coward! You dare not shoot!

Eugene. [*Leveling pistol on her.*] I will give you one minute to decide; be my wife, or meet your doom.

Sibelle. No; though twenty assassins, like yourself, were pointing their murderous weapons at my head, my answer would be the same; woman as I am, I defy you—you dare not shoot!

Eugene. [*Lowers pistol.*] Well, you are a cool one.

Sibelle. It is not coolness that braves a coward. Does this harmonize with your solemn protestations of love? I will quote your words that you uttered when we stood in the silvery light of the silent moon, and the stars of high heaven looked down to witness the workings of your deceitful heart, which would shame the infernal imps, and brand you liar! Listen! such a sermon will not hurt you:

"Love is the reflection of God in man.

No wrong motive is actuated by love;

And, when passion rules the hour,
Love takes its flight."
Eugene. You have a very retentive memory to quote so accurately.
Sibelle. It seems that *you* have not; ah, sir. I charge you, spur your memory; you are too forgetful. Mind your tongue; 'tis treacherous; 'twill shame you.
Eugene. Lady, shame and I have long been strangers.
Sibelle. Here is another of your sentimental effusions :
" When night takes the place of day,
And the silent stars their vigils keep,
And the tinted lilies bathe in the dews of heaven,
Our dreams will be of each other.
Then, in the sleep of death, where dreams are not,
In love we'll live in eternal bliss."
Eugene. [*Tauntingly.*] My pretty bird, when I take you to wife,
And your head is pillowed on this bosom,
Your drooping eye lashes closed in sleep,
And the dancing moonbeams steal in
And heighten the lustre on your silken hair,
I fear our dreams will *not* be of *each other.*
Sibelle. How could you, having the face and form of man,
Don the garb of piety, and use such holy
Means for base deception. I should think
The workings of a stinging concience
Would be terrible.
Eugene. Ah, madam, 'tis my profession.
Sibelle. You have learned your profession well.
But it has failed you this time. Foiled
In your little game—foiled—ha, ha, ha!
Eugene. Woman! Your words are like a two edged sword
That cuts on either side. I pray you have a care,
Lest that scornful laugh be superseded by bitter tears;
The reflection of a heart in torturing misery.
Sibelle. Ah! why so?
Eugene. I have other means better suited to my purpose,
Which will make you writhe and wriggle with your spleen,
And swallow your cutting words until they choke you.
Sibelle. Cease your prattle, you barking monkey!
To prate out silly nothings; your fuming threats
Will injure naught but you. I beg of you,
Smother your ill humor; 'tis not becoming to one so gallant.
Eugene. Woman, know the worst. The canker worm *secret,* is gnawing at your heart, and will not give you rest; you must answer for your husband; your hands are stained with his blood.   [CLARENCE D. *in* F.

Sibelle. Now, merciful heaven, defend me!
Spirit of the departed, hover o'er
And protect me from this vile monster!
Eugene. Ah, you do not laugh now.
Sibelle. [*Bowed at his feet.*] Oh, sir, spare me—spare me—
have mercy!
Eugene. Bowed at my feet at last.
Sibelle. Yes, yes, a thousand times yes; you will not expose
me?
Eugene. If you consent to be my wife, I will not.
Sibelle. Oh, sir, have some mercy—have some pity—if you
have a sister, think of her in my condition. I could not
make you happy—do not ask me to be your wife!
Eugene. That you must be.
Sibelle. Have you no feeling? Have you a heart? Can
you not be induced to release me? Will nothing suffice? Is
there no alternative?
Eugene. No; do you consent?
Sibelle. Oh, kill me and end my misery.
Eugene. Do you consent?
Sibelle. Have you no heart?
Eugene. No.
Sibelle. Is it turned to stone?
Eugene. Yes; stone—stone.
Sibelle. Can I not *hope* for mercy?
Eugene. Mercy? Talk not to me of mercy;
Talk to the winds, to the moon, the stars;
Talk to any thing, not human, and it
Will as soon have mercy. For the last
Time I ask, do you consent?
Sibelle. Yes.
Eugene. Then I will go for a minister immediately.
Sibelle. What, so soon?
Eugene. Yes; this very night.   [*Clock strikes one.*
Sibelle. One o'clock; but this is morning.
Eugene. This morning, then.   '   [*Starts to leave room.*

Enter CLARENCE, D. *in* F.

Eugene. What! Mr. Summerfield?
Clarence. Yes; Mr. Summerfield. I have a little settle-
ment with you
Eugene. Sir, explain.
Clarence. You are in possession of this lady's secret. Now
sir, *why* do you compel my sister to marry you?
Eugene. [*With surprise.*] Your sister?
Clarence. My sister!
Eugene. [*With emphasis.*] Your sister?
Clarence. Yes, *my* sister!
Eugene. I do not choose to explain.

Clarence. Then, sir, as I have said before, I will have satisfaction. [*Throwing glove at him.*] Accept that, you insignificant puppy.

Eugene. Do I understand that this means a challenge- that it means knives?

Clarence. Yes; knives to the hilt—to the hilt!

Eugene. I do not accept.

Clarence. In that case, you black hearted coward, the weapons shall be pistols, the time shall be whenever we meet again—at sight. [*Pointing pistol at him.*] I will give you one minute to decide. Do you agree?

Eugene. [*Bowing and starts to leave.*] I do.

Clarence. One moment. [EUGENE *stops.*] Remember, at sight. Clarence Summerfield is a man of his word, and if you have not the courage to stand up and fight like a man, I will shoot you down as I would a dog.

[*Exit* EUGENE D. *in* F.

Clarence. Sister, I overheard your conversation, and I could hardly refrain from shooting the villain on the spot. This, then, is your secret?

Sibelle. Yes; and now I must tell you that I am not your sister. I thought you were Will Hastings, from the letter and my mother's picture, that you had in your possession. I could not tell you before, for reasons best known to myself, and I can trust the secret with you, for you have always stood high in my estimation.

Clarence. I see it has been a mistake. Your secret is safe with me; but I cannot endure the thought that you are not my sister, and compelled to be his wife. Oh, Sibelle, be my wife. I love you.

Sibelle. I cannot trust my secret with him. I could not endure it to be pointed out as a murderess, or even for being tried for murder. Were it not for that, I would consent.

Clarence. This is too much to bear!

Sibelle. Clarence, you must not endanger your life for me; I am not worth it. Were I free from this man, I could not make you happy with this dreadful secret weighing me down. Now I beg of you, do not fight that duel, will you Clarence?

Clarence. Fight? Send the bullet through the coward's heart!

[*Exit* CLARENCE, D. *in* F.

[*Light thunder and lightning.*

Sibelle. Great Heavens! Must I endure all this—drag out a miserable existence with a man whom I despise? Even his presence I abhor as a hissing viper, coiled to sting with poisoned fangs. Yet I must be his wife—Oh, horrors! I cannot, it will kill me, it will kill me!

[*Bowed in grief, on chair,* R. C., *slow music.*

[*Storm, thunder, lightening and rain.*

Enter EUGENE *and* MINISTER, D. *in* F.   EUGENE *leads* SIBELLE
R. *facing* L.

Eugene. Proceed, Mr. Howell.

Mr. Howell. Eugene, do you take this woman to be your
lawful wedded wife, to love, honor, cherish and protect,
through sickness and sorrow, prosperity and adversity, for-
saking all others, and cleaving unto her, until death do part?

Eugene. I do.

Mr. Howell. Sibelle, do you take this man to be your lawful wedded husband, to love, honor, cherish and obey,
through sickness and sorrow, prosperity and adversity, for-
saking all others, and cleaving unto him, until death do part?

Sibelle. I do.

Mr. Howell. If there be any that know any just cause or
reason why these two should not be united in holy wedlock,
they can now speak, or forever hold their peace.

After a pause, enter PARTINGTON.

Partington. Yes, I have a reason, and it is because that
man, Eugene Watson, is guilty of the murder of Nathan
Saunders, the husband of this lady. [*Producing blood stained
handkerchief.* [EUGENE *looks thunderstruck.*] Do you recognize
this, Mr. Watson?

Sibelle. Thank heaven, the mystery is solved at last !

Partington. Yes, sister; this has been my one object for the
last five years. I have at last found the guilty one. My
detective life is ended, and you are a free woman.

Sibelle. Oh, brother, how can I ever repay you?

Partington. Don't mention that.

Enter CLARENCE, 1st E. L., *and levels pistol on* WATSON.

Eugene. [*Coolly.*] I am not armed, Mr. Summerfield.

Clarence. [*Lowering pistol.*] Our agreement was to shoot at
sight ; but I will not take undue advantage of you ; I will
furnish you with a pistol. We will stand back to back, as
far apart as this room will admit ; Mr. Partington will count
three, then we will turn and fire. Do you consent?

Eugene. [*Bowing.*] I do.   [CLARENCE *hands him a pistol.*

Sibelle. Clarence, do not endanger your life, you may be
killed!   [*Exit* SIBELLE, L. D.

Mr. Howell. Yes, you may be killed—Gentlemen, I implore, desist ! [*Rubbing hands, excited.*] Oh, the scandal,
gentlemen, the scandal ! Oh, I cannot witness this affair.
[*Exit* D. *in* F.

[*They take positions.* EUGENE, R. U. E.; CLARENCE, L. 1 E.

Partington. Are you ready ?

Both. Yes.

— *Partington.* One—two—

Enter SIBELLE, *much agitated.*

Sibelle. For heaven's sake, brother, do not say the word! Forbear awhile, I beseech you! [*To* CLARENCE.] Do not stain your hands in blood! Should you triumph in this, nothing could mitigate the stinging remorse of a guilty concience! Clarence, let the law take its course.

Clarence. The law?

Sibelle. Yes; this man, Watson, is now under arrest for the murder of my husband, and I believe him guilty.

Partington. So he is.

Clarence. Sibelle, you are right. *You* are always right; and now I claim you mine forever.

Sibelle. Thine *forever.*

[*Curtain.*

THE END.